# FARMER BUNGLE FORGETS

Written by Dick King-Smith

Illustrated by Martin Honeysett

WALKER BOOKS
LONDON

Farmer Bungle was milking his cows
when Mrs Bungle put her head in
at the cowshed door.
"When you come for your breakfast,"
she said, "remember to bring me back
four pints of milk."

"Four pints of milk,"
said Farmer Bungle to
himself when she had gone.

"I'll remember that or my name's not
Bill Bungle." But he forgot.
So he had to eat dry cornflakes and
drink black tea.

After breakfast Farmer Bungle
was harnessing the pony to the trap
when Mrs Bungle put her head in
at the stable door.

"Where are you going?" she said.

"Or have you forgotten?"

"Of course I haven't forgotten,"
said Farmer Bungle. "I'm going to the mill."

"What for?" she said.

"To buy a sack of barley meal for the pigs."

"Well, when you come for your lunch,"
said Mrs Bungle, "remember
to bring me a sack of flour."

"A sack of flour," said Farmer Bungle
to himself when she had gone.
"I'll remember that or
my name's not Bill Bungle."

But by the time Farmer Bungle
got to the mill, he had forgotten.

"What was it you wanted?" asked the miller.

"I can't remember," said Farmer Bungle.

"Was it cow-cake?" said the miller.

"Or barley meal?"

"Barley meal!" said Farmer Bungle.

"Yes, a sack of barley meal. And there was something else."

"Was it chicken food?" said the miller.

"Or flour?"

"Flour!" said Farmer Bungle. "Yes, a sack of flour."

But when he got back to the farm,
he fed the flour to the pigs and
took the barley meal to Mrs Bungle.
"This is barley meal," she said and
she opened the sack. "I can't bake bread
and make cakes with barley meal!"
"Oh dear," said Farmer Bungle. "I forgot
which sack was which."
"Well, I've forgotten to get you
any lunch," said Mrs Bungle sharply.

In the afternoon Mrs Bungle went out to the hen-run to feed her hens and collect their eggs.

She took a tray full of eggs to Farmer Bungle, who was rolling a field. She put them down by the gate. "Take these up to the house when you've finished," she said.

"Why, where are you going?" asked Farmer Bungle.

Mrs Bungle said, "I am going to go and buy some flour."

"Take the eggs up to the house," said Farmer Bungle to himself when she had gone.

"I'll remember that or my name's not Bill Bungle."

When he had finished rolling the field,
he drove out of the gate. Somehow
he had forgotten about the eggs.

When Farmer Bungle came in
for his tea, he found that
there was no bread on the breadboard,
no cakes on the cake stand and
no milk in his teacup.
There was an egg cup in front of him,
but there was no egg in it.

That evening, when he had milked
the cows again, Farmer Bungle
was digging his garden.
He was feeling very hungry.
Mrs Bungle put her head
round the garden gate.

"Now," she said slowly, "when you
come for your supper, remember
to bring me a cauliflower.
Do you think you can remember that?"

"Of course I can," said Farmer Bungle.

"A cau-li-flower," said Mrs Bungle
again even more slowly.

"A cauliflower," said Farmer Bungle
to himself when she had gone.

"I'll remember that or
my name's not Bill Bungle."

But when he had finished his digging,
he had forgotten what he had to bring.
He thought about all the things
Mrs Bungle had asked for that day.
Milk. Eggs. Flour. It was something
that sounded like flour!
Was it a flower from the garden?
A rose perhaps?
"No!" shouted Farmer Bungle suddenly.
"I've got it! It was a cauliflower!"
And he set off happily
back to the farmhouse saying,
"A cauliflower! A cauliflower!"
in a very pleased voice.
"I said so!" he said to himself.
"I'll remember that or
my name's not Bill Bungle."

Mrs Bungle was in the kitchen.

She had cooked a lovely supper
for Farmer Bungle because now
she felt sorry for him.

Everything was nearly ready.

All that was needed was a cauliflower.

"Did you remember the cauliflower?"
she asked Farmer Bungle.

"Of course I remembered it."

"Well, then, where is it?"

"Oh," said Farmer Bungle. "Oh dear.
I forgot to bring it with me."

Mrs Bungle put her hands on her hips.

She looked at her husband.

She shook her head.

"One of these fine days," she said,
"you're going to forget your own name,
Henry Bungle."